Miracle in the Glass

✡ To Save a Life is to Save the World ✡

Ruthann Crosby

Illustrated by
Richard A. Cook

This book is dedicated to the children of the world—our hope for the future.

Publication Consultants

PO Box 221974 Anchorage, Alaska 99522-1974

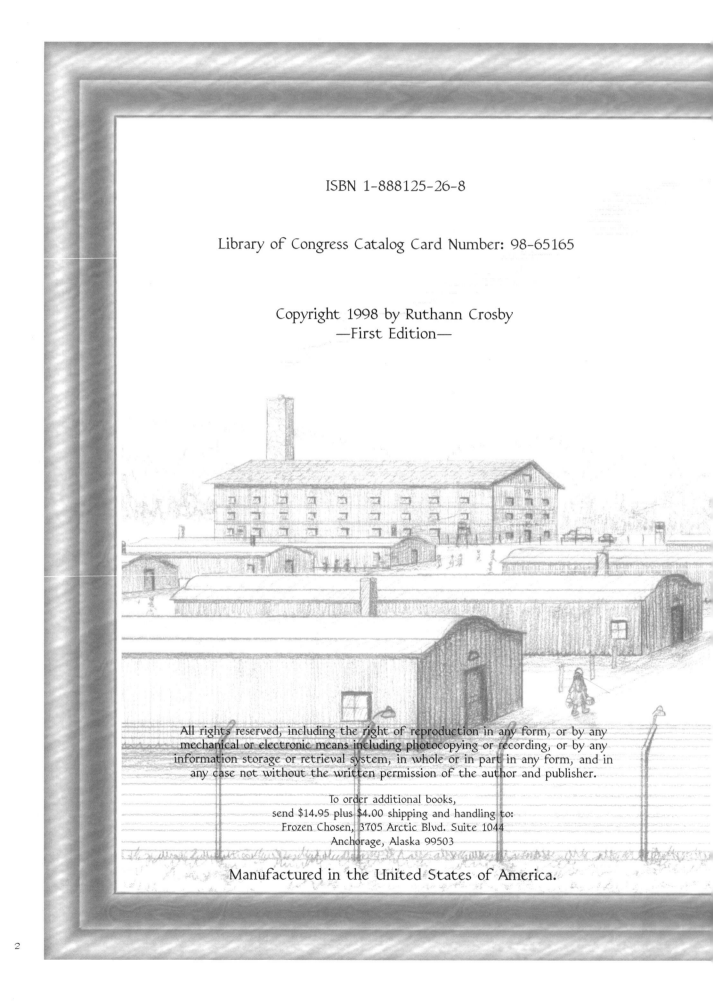

ISBN 1-888125-26-8

Library of Congress Catalog Card Number: 98-65165

Copyright 1998 by Ruthann Crosby
—First Edition—

To order additional books,
send $14.95 plus $4.00 shipping and handling to:
Frozen Chosen, 3705 Arctic Blvd. Suite 1044
Anchorage, Alaska 99503

Manufactured in the United States of America.

When I was living in Finthen, Germany, I visited Dakau. I was shocked and terrified at the experience, but while there, I noticed a woman who appeared frozen as she leaned against one of the museum pictures. Silent tears fell from her eyes. She bit her lip as she lifted her hand to touch a face—her mother or sister—I did not know. As she lifted her hand, I noticed the tattoo number. After what seemed an eternity, she pulled back and ran her fingers over the face as if to draw strength and courage from the face in the picture, although the life in front of her was no longer. She clearly mirrored the picture and somehow I left that frightening place knowing that life indeed renews itself.

On the flats outside of Anchorage, Alaska, one winter afternoon I was driving and crying. As I looked up I noticed the majesty of the mountain tops and for a split second I thought of that moment at Dakau. The Miracle in the Glass was written in my mind during that split second, showing that through the hideous crimes of the Holocaust, strength and love will prevail and with G-d there is always a miracle.

I was reminded of Psalms 17:7-8; Demonstrate clearly your kindnesses (you) who saves with your right hand those who seek refuge (in you) from those who arise (against them). Guard me like the apple of the eye; Shelter me in the shadow of your wings." *Ruthann Crosby*

Index of Hebrew and Yiddish words used in the story:

Hashem – "The Name," used to refer to G-d
      In Jewish tradition the hyphen is substituted for the letter o.
Shabbos – The Sabbath
Siddur – The Prayer book
Yoseph – Joseph
Zadie – Grandfather
Torah – First five books of the Bible
Yiddish – Language used by Jews in or from Central or Eastern Europe
Oy vey – Expression of dismay
Dreidel – Four-sided top used at Chanukah
Chanukah – Festival of Lights
"Oye Chanukah, oye, Chanukah, oye." – Jewish folk song sung at Chanukah

The sun had not yet come up over the cold concentration camp in Po-
land. Freda's hand trembled as she gently stroked Sasha's hair. Her daughter
lay curled next to her. "Would this be the day?" Freda wondered.

Rumor had spread for the last two days that the Red Army was close.
Rumors had come and gone before, but this time it seemed that the rumor
might be true. Would they finally be saved?

The German guards had doubled the marches. Day and night, long lines
of Jews were marched to their deaths.

Freda looked out the window into the darkness. She could see the
shadow of another bunker—a bunker so infested with fleas and lice
the guards refused to go near it. Inside, women were dying a slow
and painful death. Freda's heart stung.

Freda closed her eyes and continued to stroke Sasha's hair. It's
softness brought back the memory of her own mother's touch. She
heard the Yiddish voice of her mother as she sang and brushed her
hair each evening. She saw her mother light the Shabbos candles and
beckon, "Freda, Freda come! Let us light the candles." She heard her
Papa's voice reading from the Siddur.

Now she had only her daughter. If it weren't for Sasha, she would have
closed her eyes forever.

Sasha stirred. With her daughter snuggled next to her, Freda thought
of her husband and missed his warmth.

"Would Yosef recognize me now?" Her eyes were dark and hollow. Her au-
burn hair had thinned and fallen out. Sasha's tangled curls lay in her hands.

"Oh, Yosef, Sasha is my laughter and my hope. What a gift she is!
There must be a way for our daughter to live on!"

"But, it not, at least the death marches were over swiftly," she thought.

5

Three years ago in Mainz, Germany, guards pulled Freda from the basement of her family home. Hidden deep in the folds of her mother's coat, two-year old Sasha remained quiet, unseen.

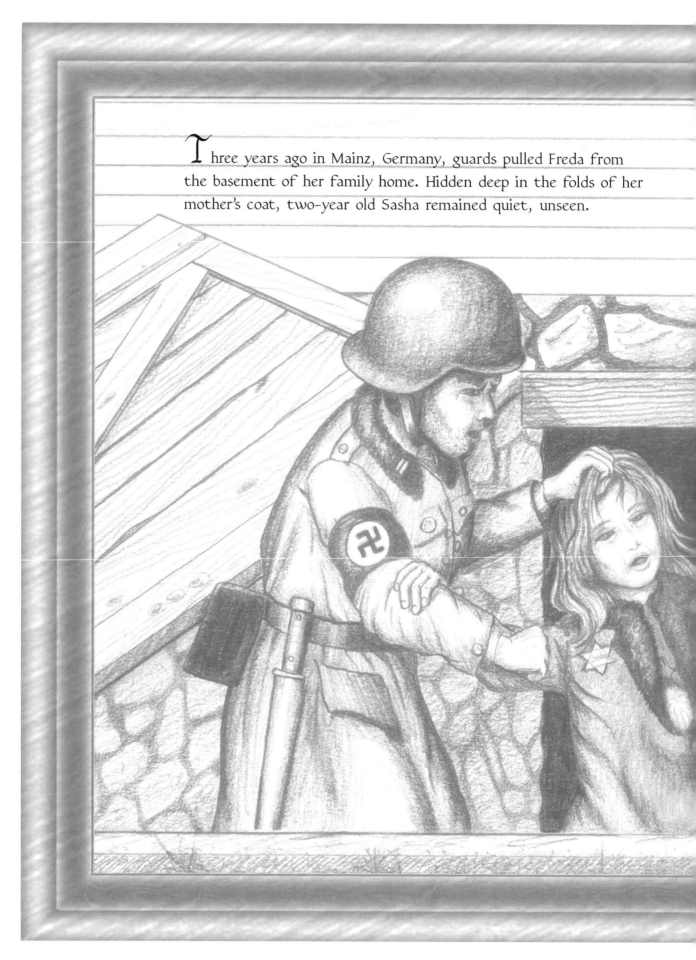

When at last the child was found, the guards threatened to rip Sasha from her mother's side. Freda believed it was Hashem, Himself, who softened their captors' hearts. Why had they allowed Sasha to stay? Freda had no answer. She only knew Sasha was a miracle.

In the camp,
Freda was diligent
to teach Sasha all
she could, as if she
were the last living
of her generation.

Freda would tell Sasha of Zadie and Papa reading aloud from the Torah and of Grandmamma bringing out the candles. She taught Sasha the old Yiddish songs.

Sasha would sing, "Maybe tonight angels will set us free!"

Every Shabbos Freda beckoned, "Come Sasha, come. Let us light the candles."

"It's hopeless. Why do you bother?" asked one woman.

"Yes, how can G-d allow us to die like rats?" whispered another. "Sasha will surely die in her youth, so what good is it? Why bother?"

"I must teach her," answered Freda. "She must learn. She must know everything."

Freda would take Sasha to the window and pretend to light the candles. They would wave their hands toward themselves over the flames, cover their eyes and recite the blessing of kindling the Shabbos candles:

Ba-Ruch A-Tah
Ado-Noi Elo-Hai-Nu
Blessed are you Lord our G-d,
King of the Universe
Who has sanctified us with
His commandments
and commanded us to
kindle the light of
the Holy Sabbath.

As the sun rose, Freda's thoughts were interrupted.

"Hurry up, hurry up!"

Freda and Sasha jumped at the sound of the guard's voices.

They dressed quickly and got in line with the other women. The guards were more irritated than usual today.

"Straighten up! Keep the line moving! Faster!"

The women were taken to work in the potato fields.

Freda found her usual place and began digging.

Sasha huddled close to her mother.

"Look!" said one of the women. She pointed to a line of coatless people marching down the road.

"Oy vey" cried a woman, "We'll be next!"

"No we won't! They need us to dig their potatoes," answered another.

"After we are all dead, they won't need potatoes," said the woman next to Freda.

"Please! Hush! Think of Sasha."

Taking Sasha's hand, Freda turned and
began to work away from the other women.

$\mathcal{F}$rost was still on the ground but the sun felt warm on their backs.

Sasha giggled, "Maybe the sun will melt us and we can be free!" She stood and lifted her face toward the sun. Freda smiled and pulled her daughter next to her as she motioned with her eyes toward the guards. Sasha understood and said softly, "But the sun does feel good, doesn't it, Mama?"

"Yes, it does." Freda looked into Sasha's big brown eyes. Even with her hollow face, the spark of life still burned within the soul of her daughter's eyes.

"Oh G-d, please spare Sasha's life!" she prayed as she watched the coatless line disappear behind the lice bunker.

The lice bunker. Freda thought of the women inside who had shared so many of her childhood memories. Mrs. Hansen and Mrs. Greenburg had often come for afternoon tea. Mrs. Stein had helped her mother with her wedding. Did they live only in her memories now?

It had been days since the German guards had thrown food at the door. The smell of death was heavy in the air. How could anyone still be alive?

Yet just last night, Freda saw movement in the bunker's window. Someone must still be alive.

Life. Hope.

Freda knew what she must do. She began to work her way through the field.

"Where are you going?" questioned one woman. "Stay in your area."

"Please," Freda begged. "Just change places with Sasha and me. I must get closer to the bunker."

"Why?"

"Please." Freda begged again. "What difference does it make?"

The woman grunted and moved aside. "Let the guards be blind," she said.

"Mama, why are we leaving our place? The guards will become angry with us."

"Hush. Stay close to me."

"You won't make it," whispered another woman. "They'll shoot you before you get to the door."

"We'll make it. We must make it."

"What door, Mama?"

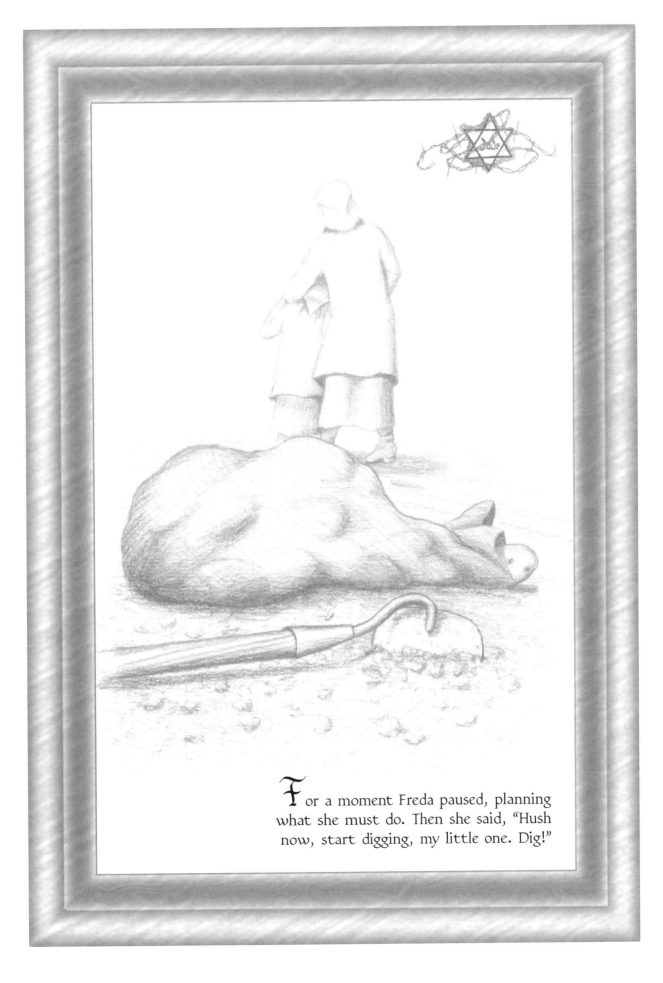

For a moment Freda paused, planning what she must do. Then she said, "Hush now, start digging, my little one. Dig!"

As they worked, Freda watched the guards march off to lunch. Only two guards remained behind to guard them, slowly making their way up and down the rows.

Freda worked and prayed. When the guards reached the far end of the field, she whispered to Sasha, "Do just as I tell you," as she began to move.

"Freda, what are you doing?" the woman behind her asked. "Please, don't! The Red Army might come for us tomorrow!"

"I must make sure for Sasha there is a tomorrow."

Energy surged through her frail body. Grabbing Sasha she raced across the field toward the lice bunker.

"Halt!" ordered a guard. "Halt!"
The sound of his boots pounded in Freda's ears.

"Open it! Open it! Hurry, open the door!" she shouted.

"Halt!" ordered the guard again.

"No!" Freda screamed. "Oh Hashem, spare my child! Open the door!" And with all her strength, she threw Sasha at the bunker.

A woman inside heard Freda's cries. Thinking it must be food, she opened the door. But instead of potatoes, a child tumbled in.

Sasha screamed, "Farvus, farvus, Mama, why? Why have you done this?" Sasha reached her hand toward the closing door. "Mama, no!"

The German guard reached Freda. He angrily beat her down. Falling, she began to sob. "Why doesn't he shoot me?" she wondered. Blood streamed down her head but with shtultz—courage—he rose shaking and walked back to the field.

The other women froze with fear and disbelief.

"Why?" whispered a woman.

"To save a life," said another.

"And if freedom doesn't come, will it not be a slow death for the little child?"

Inside the bunker of fleas and lice it was dark and horrible. Terrified, Sasha cowered to the back near the only window. With her head against the glass, tears trickled down her face. She stared out at her mother's bunker.

As evening fell, she saw Freda coming in from the fields. "Mama!" she cried.

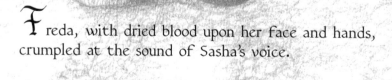

Freda, with dried blood upon her face and hands, crumpled at the sound of Sasha's voice.

The other women passed by in silence.

Freda could see the shadow of her daughter
against the window. How could she have thrown her
into such a horrible place? She would forever hear
the echoes of Sasha's screams; "Farvus, Mama, why?"
Yet, what else could she have done? Surely only Hashem knew.
Had not the energy she felt been given by Him?

"Let time be on the side of the Red Army," she prayed.

The night seemed to last forever. Alone in her bunk, Freda dug her hands into her ragged coat and wrapped it tightly around her. Deep in her pocket she felt the dreidel she had made for Sasha out of a potato. Pulling the dreidel close to her heart, she wept.

In her memory she heard Sasha's voice. She heard the voices of her own childhood: "Oye Chanukah, oye Chanukah, a Yom Tov a Shaine." Surely Hashem would keep the light of Sasha's life burning bright.

Sasha cried through the night. She felt the bites and stings of the fleas and lice, but the pain in her heart was greater. She ached for the warmth of her mother's arms holding her close.

"Farvus?" Sasha wept to herself. "Why?"

In the morning, the German guards stood rigidly outside Freda's bunker

"Come out!" they ordered. "Leave your coats!"

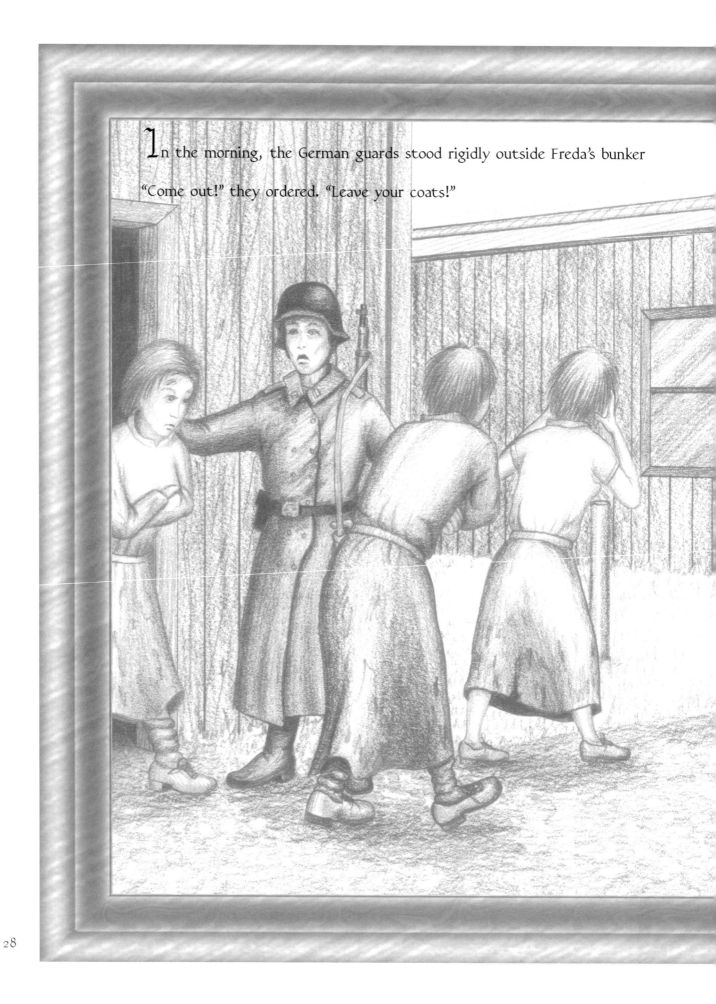

The guards were silent. They did not taunt
or tease the women as they lined up.

"March!" ordered the guards.

Freda's heart rose in her throat.

"Is Sasha still at the window?
Will I see her one last time?"

"Move!" yelled the guard.

Holding back her tears, Freda followed the others.

"I must have chozek—strength—for Sasha."

The wailing of women and the clicking of German boots against the ground startled Sasha from her uneasy sleep. She recognized the women's voices.

Panicking, she scraped at the frost on the inside of the window. She searched for her mother.

"Mama!" she cried when she saw Freda. She banged fiercely on the glass.

"Mama!"

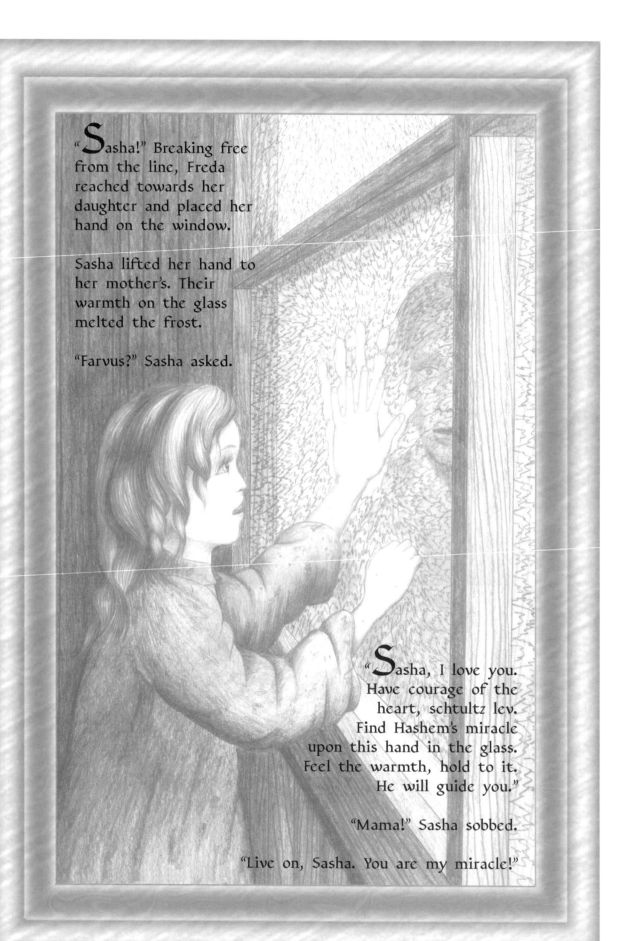

"Sasha!" Breaking free from the line, Freda reached towards her daughter and placed her hand on the window.

Sasha lifted her hand to her mother's. Their warmth on the glass melted the frost.

"Farvus?" Sasha asked.

"Sasha, I love you. Have courage of the heart, schtultz lev. Find Hashem's miracle upon this hand in the glass. Feel the warmth, hold to it. He will guide you."

"Mama!" Sasha sobbed.

"Live on, Sasha. You are my miracle!"

34

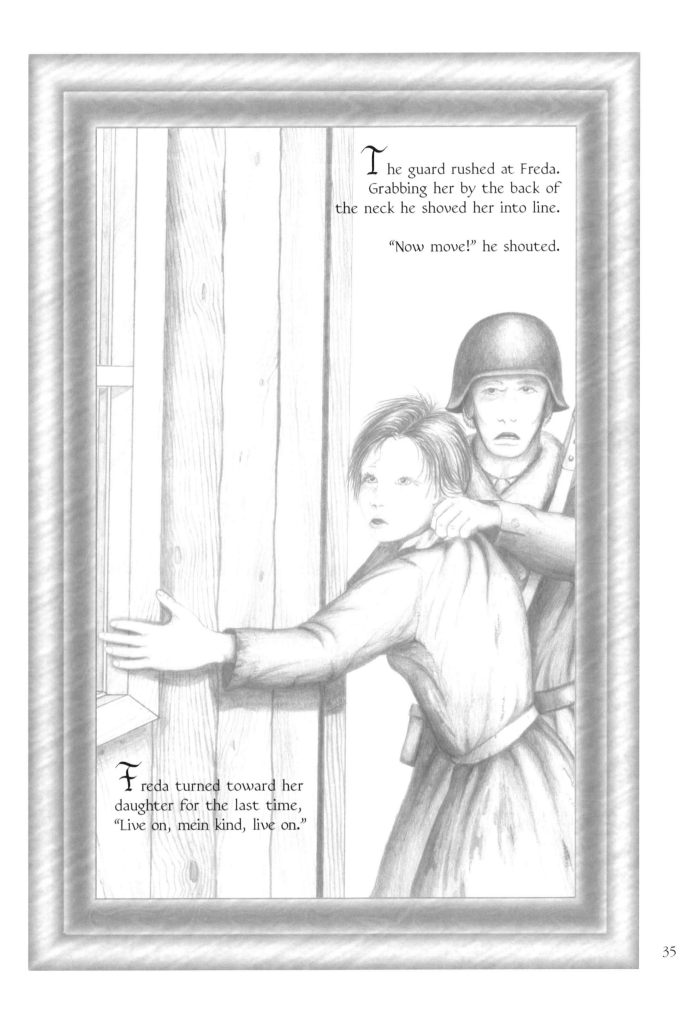

The guard rushed at Freda.
Grabbing her by the back of
the neck he shoved her into line.

"Now move!" he shouted.

Freda turned toward her
daughter for the last time,
"Live on, mein kind, live on."

Through her tears, Sasha watched her mother disappear down the road.

She held her hand to the glass. On the other side was the perfect outline of her mother's hand. Pressing hard she still felt the warmth and heard the echo of her mother's words, "You are my miracle, live on."

Minutes turned into hours. Hours stretched into what seemed like days.

Without warning, shots and loud voices broke the silence. Moments later, the door of the lice bunker was thrown open.

Soldiers cringed from the stench.

"Is anyone alive?"

The women inside drew back in fear.

"Is anyone alive?" they called again. Russian voices. The Red Army had come. Freedom!

One by one, they struggled into the morning light. "Is that everyone?" asked a soldier.

"There's a small child by the window. She won't pull her hand from the glass. She's been there since yesterday," answered a woman.

Two soldiers
went to the door.
Fleas lay like a black
blanket on the floor. "I'm
not going in there," said one.

The other soldier went to the window.
Looking in he saw the little girl with her
hand pressed to the glass. He began to tap.

Sasha screamed, "Please! No, no! My Mama's hand!"

It was then the soldier noticed the outline of Freda's hand.

Slowly, he entered the bunker and approached the little girl.

"Who are you?" he asked.

"Sasha," she whispered.

The Russian began to feel the sting of fleas on his body. "Come," he said, pulling her arm from the glass.

"My Mama's hand!
My Mama's hand!"

"Be still child." He spoke in Yiddish.

Big tears rolled down Sasha's
cheeks. "You speak Yiddish?"

"Yes, it is part of my heritage.
As a young boy, I was taken from
my family and forced into the
Russian army. Now I bring freedom to my
people." The young solder stood proudly.

Then he had an idea.

"Watch," he said. Taking a scrap
of map from his pocket he placed
it over the print on the glass.
With the sun shining through, he
traced around it. He handed the
outline to Sasha.

"Now, stand back." He smashed around
the window pane and pulled out the
glass with Freda's hand print. He
wrapped it in a piece of torn cloth.

"Here," he said.

Smiling, Sasha remembered her Mama's
words: "Schtultz Lev - courage of the heart."

She stood up straight and took the glass. "Thank you," she said. Taking the soldier's hand she turned and walked into the light.

Many years later, in a city thousands of miles away across the ocean, a little girl with deep brown eyes skips happily. Her mother looks out the window, watching the sun set on the Hudson River.

"Mama, mama," sings the child, "it's time to light the candles!" The mother nods. She reaches for her daughter and draws her close, stroking her soft, dark curls. Closing her eyes, she feels the touch of her own mother's hand. She feels the warmth of her mother's arms wrapped around her against the coldness of the camp. She hears her mother say, "Come, Sasha. Let us light the Shabbos candles and pray."

Sasha opens her eyes. "Yes, it's time. Come, Freda."

They walk to the table where two Shabbos candles have been placed in front of the outline of a frail hand print, penciled on a worn map, framed beneath a piece of old, unwashed glass.

Lighting the candles, they cover their eyes and pray.

Looking up, Sasha sees her daughter's hand print upon the glass. A tear slides down her cheek.

"Look, Mama," Freda places her little hand on the glass. "My hand's getting bigger."

Sasha smiles.
"Yes, you are growing."

Touching the glass gently, she whispers,
"Mama, I did live on. And you live on and
Papa lives on and Zadie and Grandmamma live on.
I found it, Mama. For surely, Freda is the miracle—
The Miracle In The Glass."

Special Thanks

1 wish I had words and space to thank everyone who encouraged and helped me along the way.

Mom and Dad, you taught me to never give up and always keep going. I love you.

Gary, Alan, Peggi, and families. Mr. and Mrs. Crosby, Alan, Mark, James, and families — thank you for all your help and encouragement. I love you.

Grandmother Thara Biggs Campbell Smith who loves Shabbos and showed me how important prayer is in my life.

Rabbi and Estie Greenberg for all you do for others and all I've learned from you.

Neal and Jane, Belinda and Richard, who helped me pick up the pieces and made this book happen.

Most important, Don, my husband, who has always been there, encouraging and loving me — 1 love you.

Andy, Tiffany and Gina, my children — 1 love you and am so proud of you. You have grown up to be adults with great dignity.

Sean Andrew Sablan, my grandson; Meridith Blair Wrye, my great niece; Cason Michael Alan North; Evan Christopher Bradds and Ethan Thomas Bradds, my great nephews — May Hashem's hand rest upon you and bless you always, for you are the miracles of our life